SOS PLANET EARTH

AIR SCARE

Written by Mary O'Neill
Illustrated and Designed by John Bindon

Library of Congress Cataloging-in-Publication Data

O'Neill, Mary, (date)
   Air scare / by Mary O'Neill; illustrated by John Bindon.
      p.   cm.—(SOS planet earth)
   Summary: Discusses the various forms of air pollution, how and why
they happen, and how they can be solved.
   ISBN 0-8167-2082-7 (lib. bdg.)   ISBN 0-8167-2083-5 (pbk.)
   1. Air—Pollution—Juvenile literature.   [1. Air—Pollution.
2. Pollution.]   I. Bindon, John, ill.   II. Title.   III. Series.
TD883.13.O54   1991
363.73 '92—dc20   89-49626

Published by Troll Associates, Mahwah, New Jersey in
association with Vanwell Publishing Limited.

Printed in the United States of America.

10   9   8   7   6   5   4   3   2   1

Troll Associates

About This Book...

You are growing up on a planet that needs help. Too much of its air, soil, water, and wildlife is suffering from pollution caused by humans. For many years the earth has absorbed our wastes. Now there are signs that the earth may have reached its limit.

This book takes a close look at the problems affecting our air. It has taken quite a beating from cars, industry, and the fuels we burn at home. In addition, the destruction of our forests is wiping out our most important air cleaners. You've probably heard of some of the mysterious problems caused by air pollution: the greenhouse effect, acid rain, and the attack on the ozone layer. These are all caused by what we send into the air.

In this book you'll read about how these problems are caused, where they happen, and how we can solve them. You'll also learn from Captain Conservation about some ways you can help save our air. Read on, and become part of the earth's cleanup crew!

Contents

The Air Around Us

Life on earth is made possible by a thin layer of soil, air, and water that surrounds this planet. This layer is an ever-changing balance of chemicals that we call the biosphere. All the living and nonliving things in the biosphere act together to make up the balance of life as we know it.

Take a deep breath. Your lungs have just filled with the life-giving gases we call air. But air is made up of much more than just gas. There is no such thing as a sample of "pure air." Air—even healthful air—carries solid particles such as dust from volcanoes or traces of soot from natural forest fires. And air also carries water vapor, so much at times that we can actually feel the moisture on our skin.

One of air's most important jobs is to provide living plants and animals with the gases they need. The main gas ingredients of air are nitrogen and oxygen. These normally make up about ninety-nine percent of the gas content of air. The other one percent is made up of other gases such as argon, carbon dioxide, methane, and carbon monoxide. Some of these gases are poisonous. Others can have drastic effects on our climate and environment if they are present in large amounts.

The balance of gases in our air is changed by living creatures. Simply by breathing or by changing gases into stored food, plants and animals affect the make-up of the air that surrounds us.

What's Air Made Of?

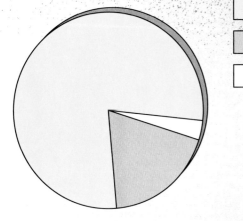

NITROGEN

OXYGEN

OZONE
ARGON
METHANE
CARBON DIOXIDE
SULFUR DIOXIDE
NITROGEN DIOXIDE
CARBON MONOXIDE

THERMOSPHERE

MESOSPHERE

STRATOSPHERE

TROPOSPHERE

Layers of the Atmosphere

The air that surrounds the earth is actually made up of different layers, like a cake. The different layers begin at the planet's surface and stretch toward outer space. Close to the earth, the atmosphere is warm and contains a lot of oxygen. The outer layers are colder. The amount of oxygen in the air decreases, too. This is why airplanes provide oxygen masks in case of emergencies.

Green Plants—Our Food and Oxygen Factories

Plants do much more than just provide shade and beauty. They make all of our food, whether we eat it as fruits, grains, and vegetables or as meat from animals. Plants also play an active role in keeping the air's gases in balance. In making their own food, plants take in carbon dioxide from the air and replace it with oxygen. We call this process photosynthesis. From a simple recipe of sunlight, carbon dioxide, and water, plants make food in the form of a sugar called glucose. This glucose is stored in the plant's leaves, fruit, or roots. When we eat spinach leaves, tomatoes, or potatoes, we are eating the plant's store of food. But plants don't need most of the oxygen produced by their food-making. So they simply "breathe" it out through their leaves.

Using Up the Oxygen

All living things seem to spend a lot of time undoing the work done by plants to produce oxygen! Like plants, we humans store glucose in our bodies. When we need energy, we have to break down the glucose. To do that, we need oxygen. And so, like all living things, we go through a process known as respiration. Respiration is the exact opposite of photosynthesis: oxygen is taken in to break down glucose into carbon dioxide, water, and energy. We use the energy to move, to warm ourselves, and simply to keep our bodies working. The carbon dioxide and water are returned to the air when we breathe out.

Air on the Move

Air isn't just constantly changing—it's always moving, too. Sometimes we feel this movement when the wind blows. Air moves because of differences in temperature. Air in the outer atmosphere is colder than air close to the earth's surface. This temperature difference causes the air movement called turbulence that we sometimes feel in airplanes.

The sun also heats the earth's surface unevenly. Around the world, this gives us our different climates. Even over a small area you can find temperature differences. This is because the sun heats land more than bodies of water. These temperature differences cause breezes to blow where land and water meet.

Movements of air are important to keeping our air healthy. They help to spread solid particles, such as smoke and ash, or poisonous gases over a wide area so they don't build up to dangerous levels. But these winds also mean that pollution created in one part of the world can pop up in faraway places.

Never-ending Cycles of Nature

You've seen how living things act to keep the air's gases in balance. But they are not the only things that affect our air. The other parts of the biosphere—water and soil—also interact with the air. Exchanges of gas, particles, and water are always happening among the different parts of the biosphere. On these two pages, we'll look at the most important cycles that affect the air's contents. For billions of years, these cycles have made life possible. It is vital that these cycles stay in balance. Even a small change could destroy many types of plants and animals.

The Carbon Cycle

Carbon is a basic building block of life. It makes up part of every living thing. Carbon moves in different forms among air, water, and soil. Living things play a role in this movement. Carbon dioxide is taken in by plants and breathed out by all living things. Carbon is also stored in the bodies of plants and animals.[A] When these living things die, the carbon in their bodies becomes part of the soil.[B] Part of the dead matter will break down[C], releasing carbon dioxide back into the air.[D]

Living matter that has died presses together in the earth over millions of years. When this happens, coal, oil, and gas develop.[E] These are called fossil fuels. When we burn fossil fuels, the carbon is released back into the air in the form of gases, such as carbon monoxide and carbon dioxide.[F]

The carbon cycle is important in keeping a healthy supply of carbon dioxide in the air for plants to use. And as we'll see, it can affect the earth's temperature.

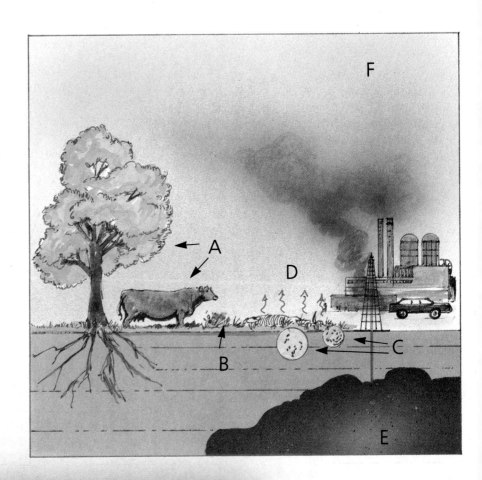

Nature's Carbon Dumps

Life in the oceans plays an important role in removing carbon dioxide gas from the air. Some types of sea creatures make shells from a form of carbon called bicarbonate. When these creatures die, the carbon in their bodies builds up on the ocean floor. Over millions of years, this can produce layers of rock called limestone. One example of such a carbon "dump" can be found along the English Channel at Dover. There, beautiful chalk cliffs tower over the ocean. They hold tons of carbon once captured from the air.

Quick as Lightning!

Nitrogen can take a direct route from the atmosphere to the soil when lightning strikes. Electricity in the air changes nitrogen to nitrogen dioxide. This falls to the earth as nitric acid when it rains.

The Nitrogen Cycle

Like carbon, nitrogen makes up part of life's smallest building blocks. Animals[A] get nitrogen from the protein in the plants they eat. Plants[B] need nitrogen to make proteins. But they can't take nitrogen directly from the air. They need the help of special bacteria called "nitrogen fixers." These "fixers" live around the roots of plants. They change the nitrogen gas into chemical forms called nitrates,[C] which can be used by the plants. Plants can then change nitrates into proteins and store them to use later.

When plants die, the proteins break down and nitrogen is set free again. Some of it escapes from the soil into the atmosphere as a gas.[D] Other nitrogen is turned back into nitrates to be used by other living plants. If the plants are eaten, the protein is stored in the animal's body. When the animal dies, its body also sets nitrogen free as the proteins break down.

NITROGEN CYCLE

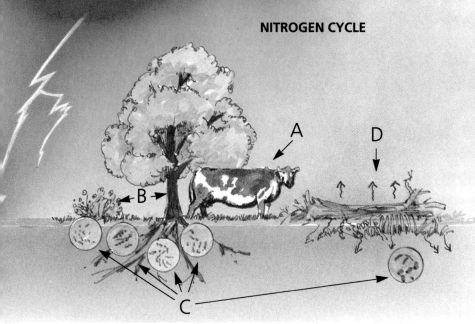

MINERAL CYCLE

The Mineral Cycle

Minerals also move through air, water, and soil. Some of these minerals, such as iron and phosphorus, are needed by both plants and animals. Minerals come from the earth first. They may enter the atmosphere when volcanoes erupt.[A] Then they are washed back to the earth when it rains.[B] Plants[C] take in minerals from the soil and pass them along to animals that eat them.[D] When plants and animals die, the minerals return to the soil.[E] The minerals may also be washed into the oceans.[F] There, they may build up over time to form new rock on the seabed.

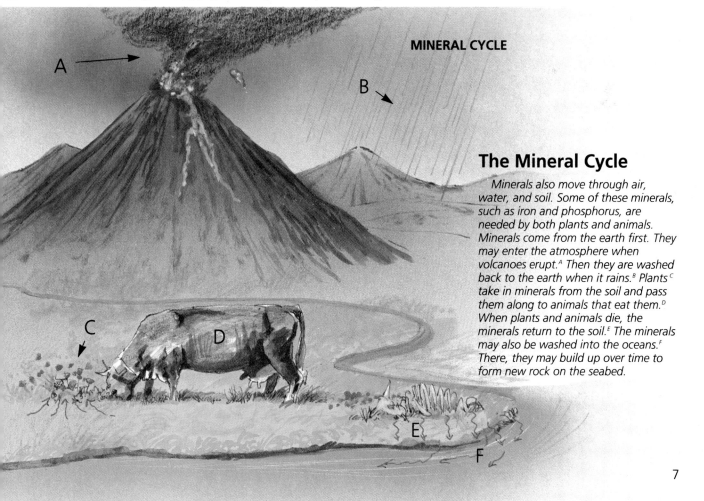

Upsetting the Balance

The natural cycles that keep our air in balance are powerful and have been at work since life first appeared on the earth. Our planet seems to have many ways of absorbing different gases and particles in the air. So why are we concerned about air pollution?

In a short space of time, we humans have had a great impact on the environment. We have been around for only a tiny fraction of the earth's history, yet scientists are finding signs that we are changing the make-up of our biosphere. The very air we breathe may be different from what it was thousands of years ago.

In the last 150 years, human activity has changed greatly. We have gone from being spread out over wide areas to living in crowded cities. We have changed the way we make things. For example, most of our products are now made by machine instead of by hand. We also travel farther and more often. All of these activities pour wastes into our air, water, and soil.

The earth has ways of adjusting to changes we make. But it adjusts slowly, over thousands or millions of years. In the meantime, plants and animals that are suited to a certain environment may die out if their surroundings change too quickly.

Fueling Pollution

The earliest humans got by using little fuel. They relied on natural energy from the sun for warmth. In the winter, they used sticks of firewood for campfires to keep warm.

As industry developed, new machines called for more energy. New types of fuel were needed to keep these machines running. People discovered the great energy store of fuels buried in the earth—coal, oil, and gas.

In the nineteenth century, coal was the most important fossil fuel. Coal fires burned in the stoves and fireplaces of most homes. Coal also made the steam engine possible. In the twentieth century, oil and gas became our main energy sources. And in recent years, more than three quarters of the energy we use comes from coal, oil, or gas.

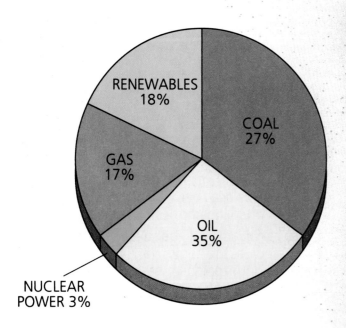

When Fuel Burns

Fossil fuels do many important jobs for us. But they are not "clean" fuels. They are carbon based. This means that when fossil fuels are burned, they release carbon into the air, along with a number of other particles and chemicals.

The burning process takes place inside furnaces at home and in factories, and inside car engines. These engines and furnaces release millions of tons of pollution into the atmosphere each year. The exact materials sent into the air depend on the type of fossil fuel burned and the type of furnace or engine. Below are some of the substances produced when fossil fuels burn.

Burning fossil fuels produce: carbon dioxide, carbon monoxide, hydrocarbons, lead particles, sulfur oxides, nitrogen oxides, ozone, and particulates (soot, smoke, metals, dust, etc.).

CARBON DIOXIDE

OZONE

HYDROCARBONS

CARBON MONOXIDE

LEAD PARTICLES

PARTICULATES:

SULFUR OXIDES

SOOT, SMOKE

NITROGEN OXIDES

METALS, DUST

Some of these substances, such as carbon monoxide or lead, are poisonous by themselves. Other substances mix with ingredients in the air and become dangerous. They can do harm to plants and animals, or they can change conditions in the environment such as temperature.

Focus on the Car

The car is one of air's greatest enemies. Pollution that comes from car exhaust pipes can cause many problems in the environment. Car exhaust causes acid rain and city smog, and may be helping to raise our planet's temperature. The processes of making new cars and getting rid of used ones also add to pollution. Workers must clear land to make room for paved roads and parking lots. This cuts back on "green space"—forests and other plant life— that is important for healthful air.

Some car engines run on leaded gasoline. These engines release lead into the atmosphere. Human bodies now contain 500 to 1,000 times as much lead as our prehistoric ancestors. Lead may cause brain damage and attack the nervous system.

Car bodies are produced by the steel industry. Steel smelters send thousands of tons of sulfur dioxide into the air each year. Sulfur dioxide is the main cause of acid rain. (See pages 16-17.)

The average car trip carries 1.3 people. A train 164 yards (150 meters) long would carry as many people as a 3-mile (5-kilometer) stretch of cars.

Car seats may be covered in a plastic that contains substances called polyvinyl chlorinates (PVCs). PVCs are suspected of causing cancer.

CFCs (chlorofluorocarbons) are eating the earth's ozone layer. (See pages 22-23.) And each time a car air conditioner is installed, 2.5 pounds (1.1 kilograms) of CFCs are released. This is because the active cooling ingredient in air conditioners is a liquid or gas made up of CFCs. The CFCs escape as they are injected into the air conditioner. One pound (one half kilogram) is released each time an air conditioner is recharged.

Car exhaust in some countries contains over a thousand poisonous substances. In industrial nations, car exhaust makes up sixty to ninety percent of air pollution. Each car releases five tons of carbon dioxide every year. Car exhaust is the main source of nitrogen oxides, which produce acid rain.

Toward a Cleaner Car

Many countries are getting tougher about pollution standards for cars. In some countries, cars must be fitted with catalytic converters, devices that clean exhaust fumes. They convert some poisons into harmless substances. Different engines can be designed to run on less fuel. Burning less fuel means producing less pollution. Engines may also be designed to run on cleaner fuels. In the future, car engines might run on electricity or hydrogen. These may be almost pollution-free.

Captain Conservation: The Cleaner Way to Go

The next time you have to go somewhere, hop on your bike or go on foot instead of asking your parents for a ride. Make it a rule not to go by car if it would take under fifteen minutes to walk. You'll get cleaner air and more exercise!

Turning Up the Temperature

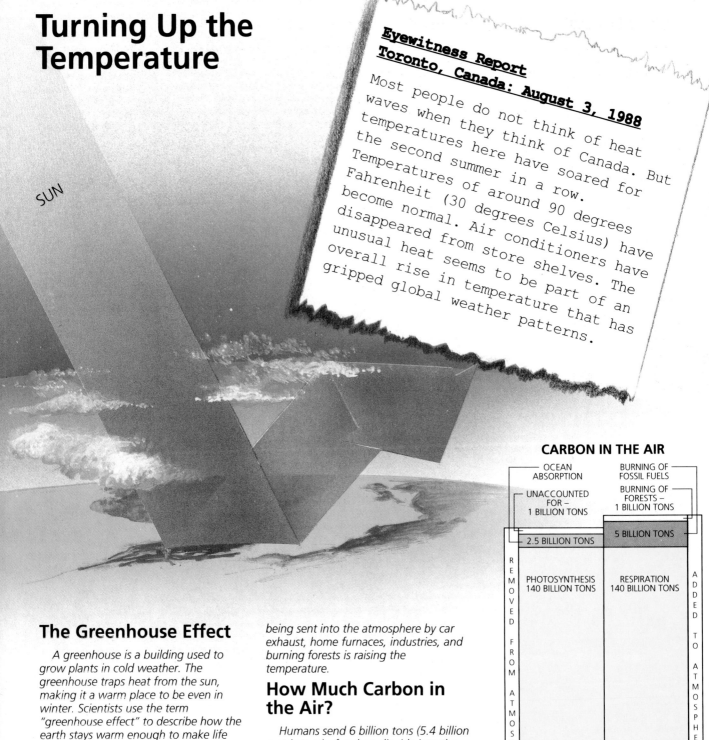

SUN

Eyewitness Report
Toronto, Canada: August 3, 1988

Most people do not think of heat waves when they think of Canada. But temperatures here have soared for the second summer in a row. Temperatures of around 90 degrees Fahrenheit (30 degrees Celsius) have become normal. Air conditioners have disappeared from store shelves. The unusual heat seems to be part of an overall rise in temperature that has gripped global weather patterns.

CARBON IN THE AIR

| | OCEAN ABSORPTION | BURNING OF FOSSIL FUELS |
| | UNACCOUNTED FOR – 1 BILLION TONS | BURNING OF FORESTS – 1 BILLION TONS |

R E M O V E D F R O M A T M O S P H E R E E A C H Y E A R	2.5 BILLION TONS	5 BILLION TONS	A D D E D T O A T M O S P H E R E E A C H Y E A R
	PHOTOSYNTHESIS 140 BILLION TONS	RESPIRATION 140 BILLION TONS	

NET INCREASE EACH YEAR 2.5 BILLION TONS

The Greenhouse Effect

A greenhouse is a building used to grow plants in cold weather. The greenhouse traps heat from the sun, making it a warm place to be even in winter. Scientists use the term "greenhouse effect" to describe how the earth stays warm enough to make life possible. Rays from the sun heat the earth's surface. Carbon dioxide and other gases in the atmosphere trap the waves of heat as they bounce off the earth's surface. This keeps them from escaping into outer space. Without this heat trap, the earth's average temperature would be as low as minus 10 degrees Fahrenheit (minus 24 degrees Celsius) instead of its natural 60 degrees Fahrenheit (16 degrees Celsius).

But when too much carbon dioxide builds up, more heat is trapped. Many scientists think that the carbon dioxide being sent into the atmosphere by car exhaust, home furnaces, industries, and burning forests is raising the temperature.

How Much Carbon in the Air?

Humans send 6 billion tons (5.4 billion metric tons) of carbon dioxide into the air each year. This is actually a small amount compared to the carbon released by respiration in nature. But the carbon released in nature is balanced by the carbon that plants take in through photosynthesis. The extra carbon produced by human activity might be more than the earth can absorb in a short time. The total amount of carbon dioxide in the air has risen by almost a third since the late 1800s. This is when people first began to use fossil fuels in great amounts.

A Hotter Future?

If we are raising the earth's temperature, what will the future hold for us? Some scientists predict that the world's temperature will rise between 2.7 and 9 degrees Fahrenheit (1.5 and 5 degrees Celsius) by the year 2030. This may sound lovely if you live in a cool region. But even a slight rise in temperature could cause problems around the world. Below are some of the ways experts think our world might be affected by the greenhouse effect in the next century.

Rainfall

On land, the amount of rain we receive might change. Some areas of the world would receive more and some less rain than now. The world's wheat-growing regions—the midwestern United States, western Canada, and the Ukraine—would probably get less rain each year. This could destroy wheat harvests, making bread a rare food.

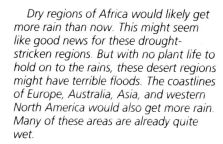

Dry regions of Africa would likely get more rain than now. This might seem like good news for these drought-stricken regions. But with no plant life to hold on to the rains, these desert regions might have terrible floods. The coastlines of Europe, Australia, Asia, and western North America would also get more rain. Many of these areas are already quite wet.

Sea Levels

A temperature increase caused by the greenhouse effect would be highest at the North and South Poles. Today these areas are locked in huge masses of ice. A rise in temperature could begin to melt these great ice sheets, sending tons of water into the earth's oceans. Like a bathtub filled to the rim, the oceans would rise and spill over onto land. Many low-lying coastal areas could find themselves underwater. Areas such as Florida, Bengal, and the Netherlands already have problems with flooding.

Wildlife

Animals that live in coastal regions depend on the special conditions found in areas where wet and dry lands meet. As ocean levels rise, their homes would be flooded. The animals would be forced to move farther inland. But human settlements and roadways would block their path, trapping them along the flooded coast.

Life underwater would suffer, too. Coral reefs are slow-growing life forms that are home to thousands of underwater plants and animals. As water levels rise, less sunlight would filter down to the plants living on the coral reefs. Without sunlight, these plants would not be able to produce food for the many animals that depend on them.

The rise in sea levels could also trigger a change in the direction of sea currents. This could change temperatures and salt levels in different regions of the sea. We can't even begin to guess the damage this might do to fish.

The Forest Connection

Part of the solution to our temperature problems is within our reach. We can turn off the heat by sending less carbon into the air and by "greening" our planet with trees and plants. Forests may be our greatest friends in nature. Each tree acts as a giant carbon-eater. Through the process of photosynthesis, trees take in carbon dioxide and release life-giving oxygen.

But instead of increasing the amount of green cover in the world, humans keep destroying forests. Millions of square miles of trees disappear each year. In the northern part of the world, almost one tree in every six is dead or dying from acid rain. But the greatest threat of all is to the huge tropical forests in the southern part of the world. About twenty million acres (eight million hectares) of tropical forest are cut down each year. Soon, these forests will be only half the size they were in 1950. To make matters worse, the trees are often burned when they are chopped down. Burning the trees adds a billion tons (900 million metric tons) of carbon dioxide to the air each year.

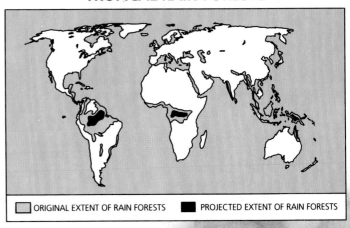

TROPICAL RAIN FORESTS

☐ ORIGINAL EXTENT OF RAIN FORESTS   ■ PROJECTED EXTENT OF RAIN FORESTS

Farming the Jungle

Ricardo Chavez looked on his withering fields in despair. After only three years of farming his freshly cleared land, the crops were beginning to fail. How could the soil that had supported rich jungle be exhausted by his small fields of corn?

Ricardo and his family had joined three other families to clear a patch of the dense Amazon jungle. Encouraged by the government that had given them the land for free, the families sweated together for nine months, cutting and burning the enormous trees and thick undergrowth. The work was hard, but the land would be their own. Back home, Ricardo and the others could find only temporary work on farms that were overcrowded and owned by others. Here, they had hopes for a better future.

The farmers did not know it, but the rich nutrients of the forest were stored in the huge trees they had eagerly burned. The soil layer underneath was thin and poor. After only a few years of being farmed, the soil was exhausted and could give no more.

Around the World: Costa Rica Saves Its Forests

Life in Costa Rica is easier than for some of its Central American neighbors. Still, this nation faces a debt of over three billion dollars. Other nations might sacrifice their forests to pay off crippling debts. But in Costa Rica, where about one third of the land is forest, the people are struggling to save their greatest resource. Costa Rica has over twenty different parks and reserves protecting thirteen percent of its land. Instead of cutting down trees, Costa Rica is looking into ways of making money from living trees. The forests' natural beauty brings thousands of tourists. Foods from the forest, such as vanilla and cacao, also earn cash. Costa Rica may prove to be a model for other nations facing the difficult choice between trees and money.

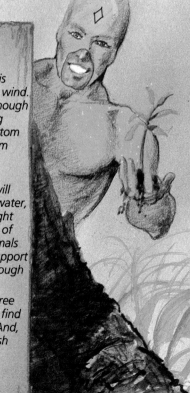

Captain Conservation: Plant Your Own Tree!

Wherever you live, you can fight air pollution by planting a tree of your own. If you don't have a yard at home to plant in, your school or local park might be happy to help you plant a tree for them.

You will be helping the environment most if you grow your tree from seed. You'll find plenty of seeds in local gardens or forests during the fall or winter. Collect a few different types and plant some of each type in a small pot of rich soil. Keep the soil moist and wait for the seeds to sprout. Be patient! Some may take up to a year. Others will appear in just a few weeks.

In the spring, choose a sapling that has grown at least six inches (fifteen centimeters). Plant it in a spot that is fairly sunny but protected from the wind. The hole you dig should be large enough to hold the roots without damaging them. Make sure the soil at the bottom of the hole is loosely packed but firm around the tree's stem. Water the sapling right away.

For its first few years, your tree will need lots of help. Give it plenty of water, especially during dry spells. You might want to surround it with a few feet of tight mesh fencing to keep out animals and wind. A small stake will help support your tree until its trunk is strong enough to stand alone.

With each passing season, your tree will bring new surprises. You might find local animals making a home in it. And, it will be helping to keep the air fresh and rich in oxygen.

Acid Rain

In the 1980s scientists set out to explore mysteries reported by people living in the Swedish province of Bohuslän. Chicken farmers in the area reported that their hens were laying eggs with thin shells. In houses, water pipes and cooking pots were corroding. And some of Sweden's blonds were finding their hair turning green! The scientists found that the local tap water was high in metals such as copper, zinc, and cadmium. By themselves, these metals were a dangerous problem. But even worse, the metals were caused by a greater threat—acid rain.

From the Smokestacks to the Clouds

Forests and lakes throughout the northern part of the globe share the problem of acid rain. Scandinavia, Canada, and the northeastern United States have been hardest hit. But even in faraway Greece, the signs of acid pollution can be seen in the crumbling faces of ancient statues.

Acid rain does not begin in the clouds—it starts on land with cars and industry smokestacks. The main ingredients of acid rain are nitrogen oxides and sulfur dioxide. Car engines are the main producers of nitrogen oxides. Sulfur pollution comes from industries such as smelters and power plants. Once these acids enter the atmosphere, the wind may blow them hundreds of miles away. Up in the clouds, the acid particles join with water vapor. They then fall to the ground along with either rain or snow.

Acid Effects

When it falls on land, the acid seems to act like a leech. It absorbs essential nutrients and minerals either from the soil or directly from plant leaves. In this way, the acid slowly starves forests to death. Half of all forests in Germany and two thirds in the United Kingdom have been damaged by acid rain and snow.

When the acids fall into lakes and streams, the whole underwater chain of life is affected. Even small changes in acid levels can kill off

important organisms such as bacteria and plankton. Bacteria are needed in the lakes to break down dead matter. This releases important nutrients into the lake. Without these nutrients, green plants cannot produce food. Plankton, the tiniest plants and animals in the water, are an important food for many water creatures. Without plankton and bacteria, many forms of water life starve to death.

High acid levels are deadly to lakes in another way. They expose heavy metals in the soil near the water. Metals such as lead, mercury, and aluminum then build up to levels that kill fish and other water creatures.

Inside a Smokestack

Scrubbers are important to air-pollution control. They can remove gases that simple screens won't catch. The most common type of scrubber uses a special liquid that absorbs gases. Instead of going up a smokestack and into the air, dangerous wastes are trapped in liquid form.

Putting a Cap on the Acid

Acid rain has to be fought at its source. It is only by cutting down on sulfur and nitrogen oxides in the air that we can save our lakes and forests. Today we have the technology to do this.

Earlier you learned that catalytic converters in cars can cut down on their harmful exhaust. And car engines can be designed to run on fuels that do not release as many nitrogen oxides. As for industry, smokestacks can be built to include scrubbers. These devices collect acids from the wastes being sent into the air.

This technology has a price, and many industries argue that the cost is too high. But as the effects of acid rain become worse, governments may be forced to deal with the problem. It is hard to put a price on healthy lakes and forests.

The Garbage Problem: Up in Smoke

In the 1980s, dock workers in Nigeria were handling some unusual cargo. Nigeria was just one of a growing list of developing countries that take toxic wastes from their neighbors. Many industrial nations today have run out of space for their garbage. Sending ordinary garbage—and toxic wastes such as chemicals—to other countries is one way of dealing with this growing mound of trouble.

More and more cities today are looking at another way of getting rid of garbage—by sending it up in flames. To some people, burning garbage is the answer to a dirty problem. Others worry that careless burning can simply change some types of garbage into other, more dangerous forms that spread through the air.

All in a Day's Waste

An average incinerator burns 1,600 tons (1,451 metric tons) of waste a day. Its stack will release 5,000 pounds (2,250 kilograms) of lead and 20 pounds (9 kilograms) of mercury. It will also produce a small number of chemical compounds called dioxins and furans. These chemicals are produced when certain wastes are not completely burned. The incinerator will release only 0.06 pound (27 grams) of these each day. But these chemicals are believed to be among the most dangerous toxins in the world. Scientists fear that even tiny amounts in the body may increase the risk of cancer.

Inside an Incinerator

When materials are burned, the chemical bonds that hold them together break down. This breakdown "shrinks" the materials, so they take up far less space. It also releases ash and gases. Some are harmless; some are not.

Garbage is burned in a special furnace called an incinerator. When natural products such as wood or food wastes are burned, their molecules react with oxygen to form water vapor and carbon dioxide. A single incinerator can add thousands of tons of carbon dioxide to the air each year.

Burning manufactured products, such as glass, plastic, or metal, can release poisonous chemicals and heavy metal particles. Some of the gases released are directly poisonous. Others add to acid rain or the greenhouse effect. Some of the metals, such as lead and mercury, are known to cause birth defects and attack the body's nervous system.

Many of these wastes can be captured by scrubbers. But because of the cost, not all incinerators are equipped with air-cleaning scrubbers. The wastes from these incinerators are released as both gas and ash. In the atmosphere, they are spread by winds and brought to earth by rain and snow.

The High-Temperature Solution?

Careless incineration can add to the problem of air pollution. But special high-temperature methods can break down difficult wastes with almost 100 percent success. If properly controlled and fitted with scrubbers, high-temperature incinerators can help solve the problem of toxic wastes.

A group of chemicals called polychlorinated biphenyls (PCBs) are one example of a "difficult" waste. PCBs were once widely used for coating and insulating. They were popular in industry until doctors and scientists linked them with cancer and other health problems. Today, production of PCBs is banned in most countries.

PCBs were so useful because they are stable—that is, they do not break down easily. So even though they are rarely made now, thousands of tons of PCBs lie waiting around the world. Only special high-temperature incinerators can properly dispose of them. PCBs must be heated to 2200 degrees Fahrenheit (1200 degrees Celsius) before they break down. If they are burned at too low a temperature, PCBs give off even more dangerous toxins, such as furans and dioxins.

High-temperature incinerators are expensive. Few of them are in use around the world. Many communities do not want them built nearby. In order to be practical, these incinerators have to process a lot of waste. This means that garbage would be shipped from other areas to the incinerator. And even though they are efficient, a tiny bit of each load escapes into the environment. With thousands of tons of toxic waste burning at these incinerators each day, people fear that their neighborhoods will suffer.

Captain Conservation: Get a Handle on Your Trash

The garbage problem begins with all of us. By cutting down on what we send to the dump, we can help the environment. The three R's to end the garbage problem are Reduce, Reuse, and Recycle:

1. You can reduce your garbage by not buying so much to begin with. Try to cut out what you don't need. And avoid things that come in too much packaging. Buy cereals in bulk, for example, instead of in boxes.

2. Reuse as much as possible. Items such as yogurt containers and glass jars can be used again and again to store things.

3. Find out about recycling programs in your area. Many cities and towns offer to collect newspaper, glass, and some types of plastic and metal. Leave these materials aside for collection.

City Air

If you live in a city of even a few hundred thousand people, you know what city air can be like. On certain days, your city may be both smelly and hazy. The air might give you a sore throat, an aching chest, or stinging eyes. Think of the fumes produced by thousands of cars and chimneys each day. Now add the chemicals sprayed by people using products such as "air fresheners" and furniture polish. This will give you some idea of what you are breathing.

What happens when all of these ingredients get together? The result is a chemical haze we call smog. The effects of smog can be either mild or severe. It can damage plants and affect our skin and breathing. In some cases, it can kill people. Weather can play its part in making smog better or worse. Weather can either trap pollution over a city or help spread it over a wide area.

The Deadly Fog of London

London is a city known for its fog. But there was something different about the fog that settled in on a cool Thursday evening in December 1952. As the city awoke the next morning, the smoke from millions of coal fires rose into the foggy air. Cars, buses, and factories belched out their fumes, too. As the day went by, the still, wet air soaked up these poisons. The fog grew darker as the day wore on. Four thousand Londoners died from breathing problems. They were victims of a type of smog that forms when sulfur dioxide and smoke particles get together in wet air.

WARM AIR

COOL AIR

Los Angeles in Crisis

Los Angeles, California, is a city that comes to mind when we speak of smog. For decades the people of this city have loved their automobiles. Los Angeles is a city of freeways, home to about eight million cars. These millions of exhaust pipes have made Los Angeles one of the smoggiest cities in the world.

The smog in Los Angeles is made even worse by natural conditions. Surrounded by mountains, Los Angeles experiences periods called "temperature inversions." Normally, cool air lies on top of warm air. When a temperature inversion takes place, the warm air moves above the cold air. This switch traps pollution beneath the warm air. Instead of blowing over a wide area, smog settles in to choke the city.

The smog of Los Angeles is different from the deadly London fog. The smog is caused by pollution from cars and industry reacting with radiation from the sun. The reaction produces a number of harmful chemicals. The whole environment of southern California has been affected by Los Angeles' smog.

Cleaner Air for Los Angeles

It will take giant steps to clean up Los Angeles' air. In the late 1980s, officials in California came up with a drastic cleanup program known simply as "the L.A. Plan." Its main concern was the automobile. Planners hope that by the end of the first or second decade of the twenty-first century, most vehicles in Los Angeles will run on nonpolluting fuels. To meet its clean-air goals,

Los Angeles will have to rely on car makers to produce new types of engines. Many of the city's cars may run on electricity in the future! "The L.A. Plan" also aimed to change shoppers' habits by banning products that are harmful to the air. The plan also called for local companies to install good antismog devices—no matter what the cost.

Planning a Clean-Air City

With better planning, cities of the future won't have to take drastic measures in order to have breathable air. Here's a model of some of the things a clean-air city might include:

Neighborhood parks provide play space for children as well as fresh air, shade, exercise, and relaxation.

Neighborhood streets that are curved or have speed bumps prevent cars from driving too fast.

Well-insulated homes heated by "clean" fuels (such as electricity or solar power) send fewer harmful fumes into the air.

Wider sidewalks lined with trees encourage people to walk more.

Bicycle paths provide another safe, clean way to get around.

Cheap and reliable public transportation means fewer cars on the road.

Weakening of the Ozone Layer

Our planet is bombarded by radiation from the sun. Without these warm rays, the earth would be a frigid, lifeless place. But too much of certain rays can be harmful to life. High above our heads is a thin layer in the atmosphere called the ozone layer. It protects us from harmful ultraviolet rays. These rays, called UV-B, are screened as they pass through the ozone layer. But now this important shield is showing signs of wear and tear.

Scientists have discovered that the ozone layer is growing thinner— even developing holes. This is allowing more UV-B rays to reach the earth's surface.

OZONE LAYER

UV-B RAYS

ATMOSPHERE

CFCs—The Spray-Can Hazard

If you're wondering what's eating our ozone, look no farther than the nearest spray can or refrigerator. Ozone is gobbled up when it reacts with chlorine released by chemicals called chlorofluorocarbons—CFCs. CFCs have brought us many modern conveniences. They are used in foam plastics, such as those used to package some fast foods. CFCs also act as coolants in refrigerators and air conditioners. And CFCs make spray cans spray.

When CFCs rise into the ozone layer, the sun's ultraviolet rays break them apart. Chlorine atoms are then released from the CFCs. These atoms react with and change ozone molecules. In fact, a single chlorine atom can change thousands of ozone molecules. And that leaves less ozone.

Sun-bathers Beware!

A "healthy tan" is getting to be quite unhealthy. UV-B rays damage skin cells and increase the risk of skin cancer. As the ozone layer thins, our skin receives more of these damaging UV-B rays. Radiation also attacks the body's immune system. This means that our bodies are less able to fight off disease.

Sun-bathers aren't the only victims of UV-B rays. Plant cells are also damaged by greater doses of these rays. Scientists fear crop failures if the ozone layer thins too much over farming areas.

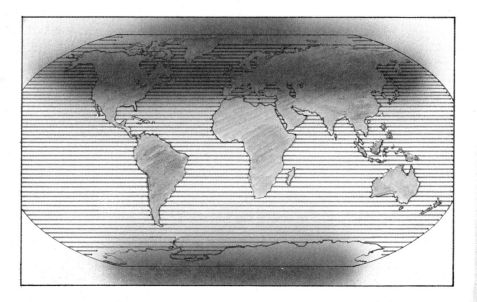

The greatest damage to the ozone layer seems to be over the North and South Poles. In 1985 an ozone "hole" was discovered over Antarctica. The hole is affected by wind patterns that shift with the changing seasons, so it is not always the same size. In 1989 scientists discovered that an ozone hole might also be developing over the Arctic pole. The farming regions of the mid-Northern Hemisphere may be affected, too. Their skies lost 1.7 percent to 3 percent of their ozone between 1970 and 1988.

Cutting Off the CFC Supply

As the ozone problem becomes clearer, many industrial nations are cutting back on the production of CFCs. But while they cut back, some nations are only beginning to use CFCs. China, for example, plans to produce much more CFC. This is because more and more people in China want refrigerators. Nations working to limit CFC use will have a tough job convincing poorer nations. Some can just afford modern conveniences such as refrigerators for the first time.

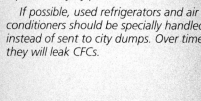

Captain Conservation: Saving the Ozone Layer

Here are a few things you and your family can do to protect our ozone layer:

Say "no thanks" to styrofoam packaging. CFCs are released when styrofoam breaks down. If your favorite fast food comes in this packaging, look around for another brand that doesn't.

Don't use aerosol sprays. Many products such as deodorants come in other forms that are just as easy to use.

Air conditioners at home and in cars should be checked to see if they are leaking CFCs. The coolant should be replaced only by professionals.

If possible, used refrigerators and air conditioners should be specially handled instead of sent to city dumps. Over time, they will leak CFCs.

What We Spray on What We Eat

Chemicals in the air take one path into our bodies when we breathe. When we spray these chemicals directly on our foods, we give them another path to take. To keep fruits and vegetables free from weeds and insects, most farmers spray them with chemicals called herbicidse and pesticides. Herbicides and pesticides kill the weeds, fungi, or insects, while leaving the crops alone.

But the weeds and pests develop defenses against the sprays and become harder to kill. Each year, farmers spray their crops with more of these chemicals, which do not all wash off. Traces of the chemicals remain in the foods we eat. As we digest the fruits and vegetables, the herbicides and pesticides are stored in our body fat. Some of these pesticides have been linked to cancer and other serious illnesses.

Risk-Free Eating

Your body needs fruits and vegetables. You suffer a greater risk from not eating these foods than from the herbicides and pesticides on them. Washing the outside of the foods with soap and water and rinsing them well will cut down on any sprays. If you are concerned about herbicides and pesticides, here are the best ways to handle some of your favorite fruits and vegetables.

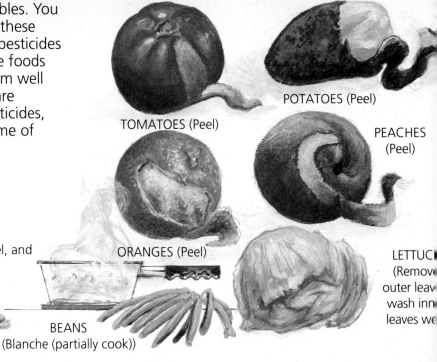

TOMATOES (Peel)

POTATOES (Peel)

PEACHES (Peel)

ORANGES (Peel)

LETTUC(
(Remov(
outer leav(
wash inn(
leaves w(

CARROTS (Wash, peel, and cook)

BEANS
(Blanche (partially cook))

Working With Herbicides and Pesticides

Farm workers who grow fruits and vegetables have even more cause to worry about herbicides and pesticides. Over long periods they may develop serious health problems such as cancer. Farm workers in some countries have been poisoned when fields were sprayed as they worked in them.

On occasion, dangerous chemicals have accidentally leaked from factories that make herbicides and pesticides, too. And a few of these leaks have been deadly.

Eyewitness Report
Bhopal, India: December 3, 1984

Officials have been unable to confirm the number of people killed in yesterday's gas leak at a pesticide plant in Bhopal. But it is feared that over 2,000 may have died already. Thousands of others are critically ill. Over thirty-three tons (thirty metric tons) of a poisonous chemical are believed to have leaked. The highly toxic chemical is used in the production of pesticides.

Chemical-Free Farming

Today many farmers are changing the way they grow foods. Instead of treating the soil with chemical fertilizer and then spraying herbicides and pesticides, they use natural growing methods. These natural methods are known as "organic" farming. Organic methods depend on careful attention to the soil and on growing a wider variety of crops to discourage weeds and pests.

To keep the soil rich, organic farmers use natural fertilizers. These are made from manure and from compost (vegetable matter that has been left to rot). Every few years each field is given a rest so that it can rebuild its natural store of nutrients. Crops are also rotated. This means that each year, a different type of crop grows in each field. Rotating crops has another advantage. Pests that lay their eggs on a certain type of plant don't get a chance to take hold. When the eggs hatch in the fields the next

spring, the young insects find themselves surrounded by a different plant—hopefully one they can't eat.

Many developing nations find another advantage in organic farming. Natural methods are cheaper. Expensive chemicals are replaced by natural wastes. Organic farming also encourages farmers to keep at least a few animals for manure. This means that small farmers can supply their own meat and vegetables.

Danger on the Wind

Air masses do not respect the borders between countries. The wind currents that circle our planet can spread pollution from one country to others. This means that we all have an interest in what our neighbors are doing. A disaster, even faraway, can affect our daily lives.

Radiation's Effects

The accident at Chernobyl killed many people. Hundreds of others suffered from a disease known as radiation sickness. Winds carried radioactive particles—the fallout—as far west as Ireland and eastern France. Heavy rains over some regions soaked local crops in radioactivity. As radioactive grass was eaten by grazing animals, their meat was infected by radiation. Several countries were forced to ban the sale of sheep and cattle.

One of the hardest-hit regions was northern Norway, Sweden, and Finland. This is the traditional home of the roaming Lapp people. For centuries, the Lapps have made their living by herding reindeer. Their whole way of life is now in danger. Tests on reindeer in the late 1980s showed levels of radioactivity seven times higher than before the accident at Chernobyl.

Because the effects of radiation are still being discovered, scientists aren't sure how such an accident will affect humans in the future. Radiation can cause body cells to change. This raises the risks of cancer and increases the number of birth defects.

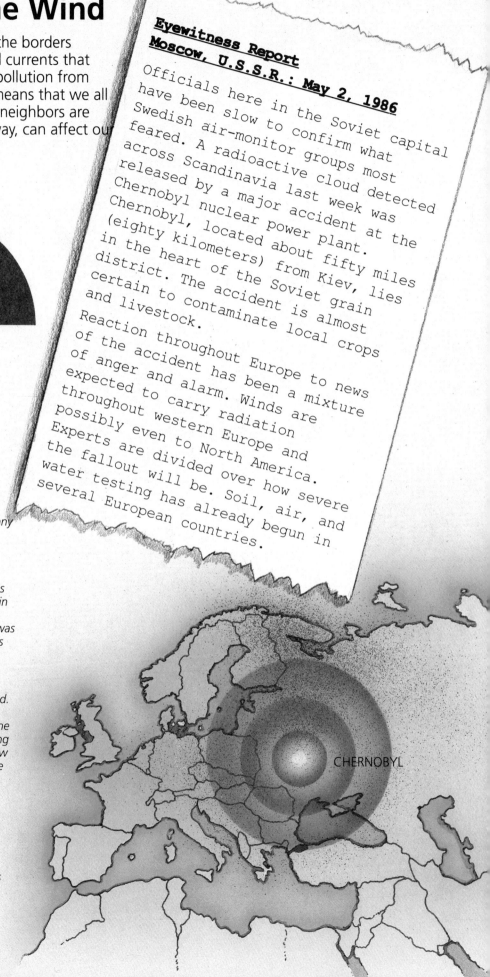

Eyewitness Report
Moscow, U.S.S.R.: May 2, 1986

Officials here in the Soviet capital have been slow to confirm what Swedish air-monitor groups most feared. A radioactive cloud detected across Scandinavia last week was released by a major accident at the Chernobyl nuclear power plant. Chernobyl, located about fifty miles (eighty kilometers) from Kiev, lies in the heart of the Soviet grain district. The accident is almost certain to contaminate local crops and livestock.

Reaction throughout Europe to news of the accident has been a mixture of anger and alarm. Winds are expected to carry radiation throughout western Europe and possibly even to North America. Experts are divided over how severe the fallout will be. Soil, air, and water testing has already begun in several European countries.

CHERNOBYL

Chernobyl Not Alone

Chernobyl[1] was a terrifying accident that has made us take a closer look at the safety of nuclear plants. Since the late 1950s there have been three other <u>major</u> nuclear accidents around the world: Kyshtyn[2], U.S.S.R. (1957/58); Windscale[3] (now known as Sellafield), Britain (1957); Three Mile Island[4], U.S.A. (1979).

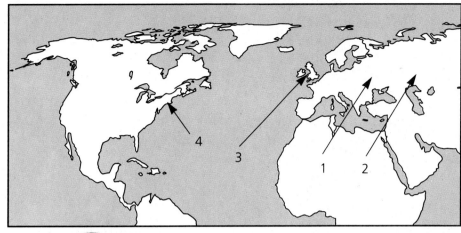

How the Body Absorbs Radioactivity

Radioactive fallout is made up of a number of different substances. All may be taken in by eating, drinking, or breathing. But each substance is absorbed and stored in different parts of the body.

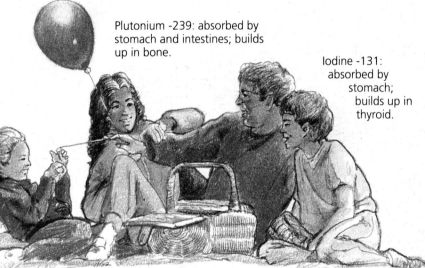

Plutonium -239: absorbed by stomach and intestines; builds up in bone.

Iodine -131: absorbed by stomach; builds up in thyroid.

Cesium -134/137: absorbed by intestines; builds up in muscles.

Strontium -90: absorbed by intestines; builds up in bone.

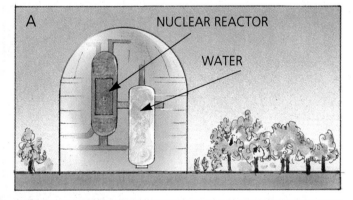

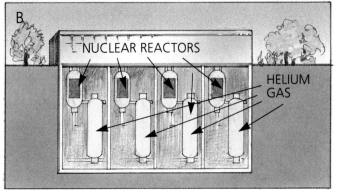

Toward a Safer Reactor

In spite of its dangers, more and more of our future energy may come from nuclear power. The accident at Chernobyl and several other leaks have shown the importance of safer plants.

Today's nuclear power plants are mostly single large reactors cooled by water.[A] If the cooling system fails, the entire reactor can melt down. When this happens, dangerous radioactive material leaks into the environment. One new design calls for power plants made up of a number of smaller reactor units.[B] These "little" reactors would use nuclear fuel in such small amounts that they would not melt down. Also, the units would be cooled by helium gas instead of water. In case of a power failure, the gas would continue to cool the reactors.

Air Pollution Around the World

Many types of air pollution we've discussed begin in areas of heavy traffic and industry.

But the effects of this pollution are felt around the world. Because of the way air moves, we share our pollution with other countries. The earth's atmosphere is a delicate blanket. It can be easily damaged thousands of miles from the pollution's source.

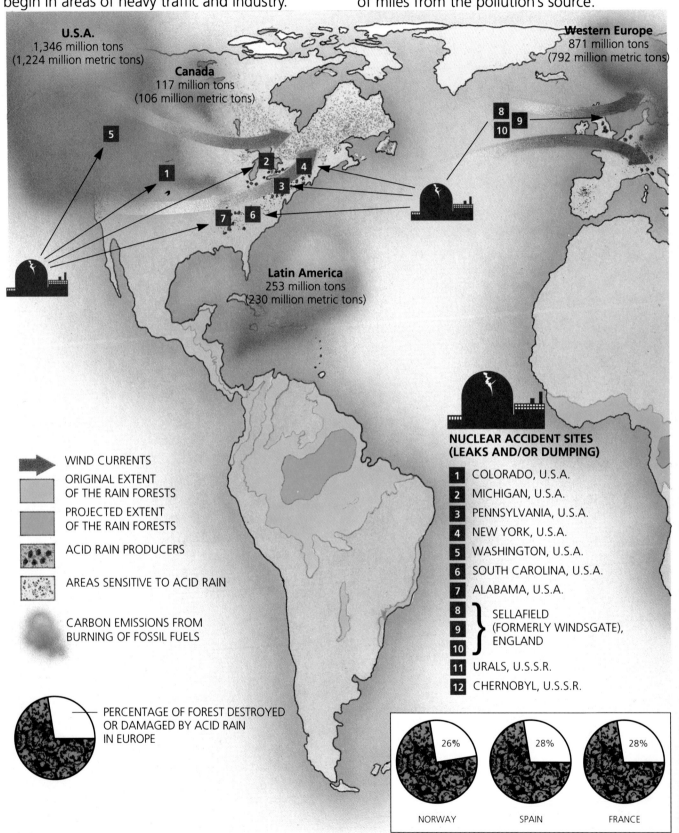

U.S.A.
1,346 million tons
(1,224 million metric tons)

Canada
117 million tons
(106 million metric tons)

Western Europe
871 million tons
(792 million metric tons)

Latin America
253 million tons
(230 million metric tons)

WIND CURRENTS

ORIGINAL EXTENT OF THE RAIN FORESTS

PROJECTED EXTENT OF THE RAIN FORESTS

ACID RAIN PRODUCERS

AREAS SENSITIVE TO ACID RAIN

CARBON EMISSIONS FROM BURNING OF FOSSIL FUELS

NUCLEAR ACCIDENT SITES (LEAKS AND/OR DUMPING)

1 COLORADO, U.S.A.
2 MICHIGAN, U.S.A.
3 PENNSYLVANIA, U.S.A.
4 NEW YORK, U.S.A.
5 WASHINGTON, U.S.A.
6 SOUTH CAROLINA, U.S.A.
7 ALABAMA, U.S.A.
8 }
9 } SELLAFIELD (FORMERLY WINDSGATE), ENGLAND
10 }
11 URALS, U.S.S.R.
12 CHERNOBYL, U.S.S.R.

PERCENTAGE OF FOREST DESTROYED OR DAMAGED BY ACID RAIN IN EUROPE

26%
NORWAY

28%
SPAIN

28%
FRANCE

The map on these two pages shows both the sources and the effects of some of our worst air problems.

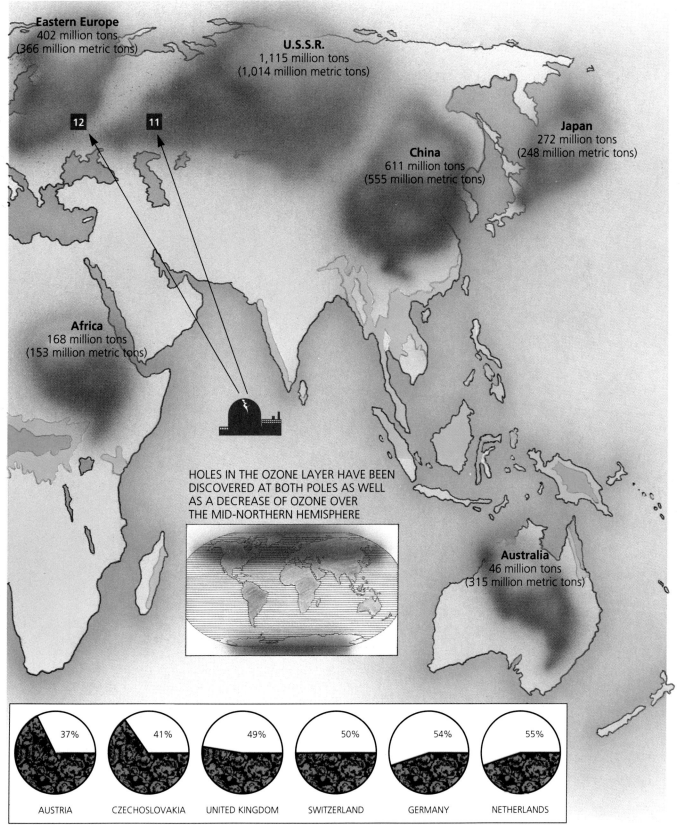

Eastern Europe
402 million tons
(366 million metric tons)

U.S.S.R.
1,115 million tons
(1,014 million metric tons)

Japan
272 million tons
(248 million metric tons)

China
611 million tons
(555 million metric tons)

Africa
168 million tons
(153 million metric tons)

HOLES IN THE OZONE LAYER HAVE BEEN DISCOVERED AT BOTH POLES AS WELL AS A DECREASE OF OZONE OVER THE MID-NORTHERN HEMISPHERE

Australia
46 million tons
(315 million metric tons)

37% AUSTRIA

41% CZECHOSLOVAKIA

49% UNITED KINGDOM

50% SWITZERLAND

54% GERMANY

55% NETHERLANDS

Cleaning Up Our Act

Like all pollution, our air troubles are caused by billions of people, each adding a little bit. Since we all take part in polluting the air, it will take all of us to clean it up. Science will not provide us with an easy solution to clean up our air. The only real solution is to change the way we act.

The first step is to realize that we take part in pollution by what we do and what we buy. Industry's pollution is just a by-product of making the things people want. If we did not demand these goods and services, they would not be produced.

Destroying materials we've used is another major cause of pollution. Everything we throw into the garbage will end up being buried or burned somewhere. So it is important to cut back on the amount we waste.

Right now, you might only be spending your money on movies, comic books, and snacks. But in ten years or so, you will be faced with decisions about a whole range of products from cars to groceries. Spending your money only on goods that are necessary, last a long time, and don't cause pollution will be one of the best things you can do for our environment.

Getting Started Today

In this book Captain Conservation has shown you some ways of helping to clean up the air. You can get started right away with tree planting, recycling, walking, or riding your bike. And you can avoid products that are made with CFCs. Here are a few more things you and your family can do to help keep our air fresh:

Save trees and reduce your garbage by using cloth instead of paper for some things. Paper towels, diapers, coffee filters, handkerchiefs, and napkins are just a few examples.

Cut down on gases that add to the greenhouse effect by saving energy at home. Keep the thermostat at 68 degrees Fahrenheit (20 degrees Celsius) or cooler. Instead of regular light bulbs, use fluorescent ones, which require less energy. Where possible, use a fan instead of an air conditioner. Fans use less energy and do not contain CFCs.

Cut down on trash by collecting returnable bottles around your neighborhood. You might make a little money by doing this, too.

Join or start a group of other young people who care about the environment. You can learn more and do more when you're all working together.

Index